The Night Heroes:

Broken Brotherhood

by
Dr. Bo Wagner

Word of His Mouth Publishers
Mooresboro, NC

All Scripture quotations are taken from the
King James Version of the Bible.

ISBN: 978-1-941039-99-1
Printed in the United States of America
© 2014 Dr. Bo Wagner (Robert Arthur Wagner)

Word of His Mouth Publishers
Mooresboro, NC
www.wordofhismouth.com

Dedication

This book is unique in that it is dedicated in memory and honor of a man that I have never met. Yet, despite the fact that I have never met him, I know that I owe him a great debt of gratitude. The late Burman Cape is one of the old heroes of the faith, a man of God that paved the way for younger preachers like myself.

The Reverend Burman Cape, Sr. was saved on September 18, 1946. He answered the call to preach shortly thereafter. Although he didn't publically proclaim his call to preach that night, he always said he believed that God saved him and called him to preach the same night. Brother Cape's ministry covered a span of some 64 years, having spent over 50 years as a pastor.

He founded two churches: the Hinton Baptist Church of Hinton, Georgia, and the Bible Baptist Church of Rossville, Georgia, where he served for 37 years until he retired from the pastorate in 1998.

Brother Cape also preached hundreds of revivals throughout the southeast. Hundreds of people were saved over the years, but one of his most memorable revivals was in the late 1940s when he went back to Hinton, Georgia, where he grew up as a boy and conducted a revival under an old arbor. Fifty-three people were saved and out of this revival was born the Hinton Baptist Church, which he founded, and the church still remains to this day in Hinton, Georgia.

Brother Cape was 78 years old when he retired from the pastorate and said, "I'm not retiring, I'm just re-firing." And that he did. Brother Cape and Sister Evelyn, during the next 12 years, logged over 250,000 miles traveling throughout the southeastern United States preaching the gospel and singing the familiar theme song of their lives, "God's Wonderful Book Divine."

His life can best be described by the words of the Apostle Paul, "I have fought a good fight, I have finished my course, I have kept the faith."

I chose the names George and Patrick Cape as the young preachers in this book because of Brother Cape.

I hope that this dedication and this book will be a blessing to Mrs. Cape, who is still faithfully holding high the blood-stained banner.

Chapter One

A few uneventful weeks of revival meetings had come and gone. By uneventful I mean during the nights of sleep that came after the meetings, not the meetings themselves. The meetings, praise the Lord, had been very eventful. Several people came to know the Lord during the two week revival at the Bethany Baptist Church in Thomasville, North Carolina. A couple more did the same at Lighthouse in Pageland, South Carolina, and one young man about my age surrendered to the call to preach! So no, the meetings had not been uneventful, only the nights of sleep after the meeting.

But I suppose I need to explain myself.

Our nights of sleep have been rather, well, "active" lately. A better way to put it might be "odd." Now that I think about it, considering the entire "yanked back in time to the West Virginia coal mines of 1912 to rescue a little boy before heading for Nazi Germany of World War II to jump out of an airplane to save a girl from death in the Ravensbruck Concentration Camp" thing, I suppose "excessively weird" might even be an accurate description.

Oh, and I am fourteen years old.

My sister, Carrie, is twelve.

Aly, my other sister, is eleven.

We are not just normal kids, we are *The Night Heroes*.

My name is Kyle Warner. My sisters and I are PKs, preacher's kids. Specifically we are an evangelist's kids. There are lots of evangelists and evangelists' kids out there, but I am pretty sure there are none quite like us. When we fall asleep at night while we are out in a meeting somewhere, we wake up back in the past somewhere to serve the Lord by helping people in need. There is way too much to explain here, I recommend you check out our first two books, *Cry From the Coal Mine* and *Free Fall.*

Our last few meetings had been in North and South Carolina. We were now heading further south and a bit west, making our way to Rossville, Georgia. Rossville is pretty near to the Tennessee line. It is also home to the Bible Baptist Church, which is pastored by a good man named Ricky

Gravely. He had been in a few meetings that my dad preached, and just last year asked dad if he would come and preach in his camp meeting. A camp meeting, in case you don't know, is a lot like a revival meeting, only there are a whole bunch of people preaching, not just one man. This one would have meetings in the morning, afternoon, and at night, and there would be some really good men there, men like Sammy Allen (one in a million, friend, one in a million), Stinnet Ballew, Joe Arthur, Barry Philbeck, Eric Brown, and others.

Rossville is also right near to the Chickamauga Battlefield, the site of a very famous Civil War battle. I know my dad. He is a major history buff, and there is not a doubt in my mind that we will visit it multiple times during the meeting.

When we finally got into the area, we went to the Super 8 in Fort Oglethorpe, Georgia, not too far from Rossville and the church. We arrived around four o'clock. Then, like a team of perfectly trained "people ants," we systematically carried everything up to room 201. Blonde-haired Aly had pillow duty, making sure the Yukon was emptied of everyone. Mom, the prettiest brown-haired, brown-eyed lady ever, and she really is a true lady, checked us in. Carrie, raven-haired, quick-witted, and utterly completely brilliant, handled the computer bags. I rounded up a luggage cart and had no trouble hoisting our largest suitcases out of the back of the vehicle and onto it. I even flexed a bit in front of my dad. I am strong for fourteen, very strong, but dad pretends not to be impressed. He simply rolled up one of his sleeves, flexed an arm that looked like a python, and said, "Keep working at it, Twinkie, one day you'll have real muscles!" Then I saw very white teeth shine out from under his black mustache, and I grinned right back. Together we got the vehicle emptied, the room arranged (as almost always, mom and dad in one bed, the girls in another, me in a sleeping bag on the floor) and the air conditioner turned way down low. Dad likes to make it snow. Inside.

When mom got into the room, we began the mad dash to get ready for service. The girls puffed and pampered and primped and perfumed. We men combed hair and polished shoes and tied ties and then, with that difficult five minutes out of the way, waited for the girls to finish in, most likely, another hour or so. Dad says not to bother to try and hurry them up, it will only make things worse.

Finally they were done, and we were headed out the door, down the two flights of clangy metal stairs, into the Yukon, revving the engine, putting the vehicle in gear, and heading for the church.

We got to the Bible Baptist Church in Rossville around 5:15 for supper. This is one of the best things about traveling around to meetings: these people know how to cook! We ate till we were full, but no more than that. Dad and mom have a rule, "Never stuff yourself." We all know that according to I Corinthians 6:19 our bodies belong to the Lord. If it is wrong to damage the Lord's property by smoking, doing drugs, or drinking, then it is just as wrong to damage it by overeating! Besides, the girls and I both knew now that we were going to have to stay in top physical shape to accomplish the tasks the Lord was sending us to during the night. Video-game-addicted, couch-sitting, potato-chip-eating kids would simply not be able to do the job.

Bible Baptist is a big beautiful church. And tonight there were probably 600 people packed in worshiping the Lord, praising His name. The singing was amazing. The congregation belted out the old hymns of the faith like they were brand spanking new. A great guitar player and singer named Chris Hewitt sang a special that I really like called "I Am One of Them Today." We shouted; we praised the Lord; people testified.

And then it finally came to the best time of all, the preaching time.

Pastor Barry Philbeck preached the first message, and it was really good. My dad preached last.

His message was a very serious and quiet one. It was about the crucifixion, and it was called "What Did It Cost Jesus for Us to Have a Chance to Be Saved?" People wept openly at the description of the crucifixion, and they should. I did too, even though I have heard the message before. How can anyone think of the cross and the suffering that Jesus went through and not cry?

We had two saved that night; God really moved in and did a great work. My dad's voice has been about gone for two weeks now and does not seem to be getting better, but God really helped him, and no one seemed distracted in the least.

We hung around and fellowshiped for a little while after the service. Mom and dad wanted to catch up with some old friends they hadn't seen for a while, but before too long we loaded up and headed back to the hotel. Driving for seven hours and then being in a three hour service can wear some kids out!

It didn't take long for us to get ready for bed. We all prayed together as a family, hugged and kissed one another (On the cheek. We are definitely a "kiss on the cheek" kind of family.) and then bedded down for the night. After all of the travel and all of the emotion of the meeting believe me, it didn't take us long to be sound asleep.

Or to be wide awake again.

Chapter Two

Oh, gross! Why have we suddenly become a "kiss on the lips" family? And yuck! Dad with his fuzzy beard? I am going to barf! Wait a minute, Dad doesn't have a beard; what in the world is going on? And why am I hearing giggling?

And then I blinked open my right eye, the left one was still uncooperative. But my right eye saw enough. Very long face. Lots of hair. Ears, very, very big ears. Donkey! I WAS BEING SLOBBERED ON BY A DONKEY!

As you might imagine, it didn't take long for me to be on my feet, spitting and gagging. Carrie and Aly were in the back of the wagon laughing their rotten little heads off. The Conductor was sitting in the front seat holding the reins, with a bemused smile on his face. The donkey was staring at me like I was the oddest creature it had ever seen. Well, here we go again...

"Welcome, young man," the Conductor said. "You have been sleeping very soundly, far more soundly than your sisters. But it is time for you to be up and active; your five days starts now, and, as always, the need is urgent."

"Yes, sir, I understand," I said. Then I added, "And I see that your list of driving skills just continues to grow. First it was a train, then a World War II era war plane, and now a mule and wagon. Is there anything that you can't drive?"

"Only things that I cannot drive YET," he said with another smile.

By this time Carrie and Aly had stopped laughing and were ready to get down to business.

"When are we this time?" from Aly and, "Where are we this time?" from Carrie came tumbling out at the exact same time.

The Conductor just smiled and said, "Why don't we test your powers of observation and see how close you can get. Kyle?"

"Well," I began slowly as I looked around and surveyed everything, "based on the wagon I would say that we are likely in an earlier time than we have ever been, most likely in the late eighteen hundreds. What do you think, Carrie, what conclusion has that big brain of yours come to?"

"I am thinking 1860ish," she said with no hesitation. "We are clearly still in or near Rossville, Georgia; those mountains and hills are the same ones we passed yesterday. The smell of wood smoke is in the air, but the vibrant color of the leaves tells me that it is still early fall, so I have to assume that the fire is for cooking, not for heat. Electric lighting came to Georgia in the late 1880s, but I don't see any power lines anywhere. So, yeah, I'm thinking 1860ish."

"Well done, young lady! You are, as always, incredibly observant and very logical. It is in fact the year 1863."

Carrie stopped smiling right away. That made me stop smiling. I looked over at Aly and she stopped smiling too. If Carrie stopped smiling, ever, believe me there was a reason. A bad one. We stared at her for a few silent seconds, and then she began to speak in a dreamy voice as if from long, long ago:

> "O Captain! My Captain! Our
> fearful trip is done,
> The ship has weathered every
> rack, the prize we sought is
> won,
> The port is near, the bells I
> hear, the people all
> exulting,

While follow eyes the steady
        keel, the vessel grim and
        daring;
But O heart! Heart! Heart!   O
        the bleeding drops of red,
Where on the deck my Captain
        lies, fallen cold and dead."

"Carrie, what is that?" asked Aly
quietly. "It sounds so haunting."

"It is from the poet Walt Whitman,"
Carrie said. "It is a poem about the Civil War.
If this is 1863, then we are right in the middle
of the Civil War. Every war is bad, but the
Civil War was especially bad because it was
not us against foreigners; it was us against us.
There were actually families who were so
divided that some would fight on the Union
side while others in the exact same family
fought for the Confederacy."

"And that, young lady, is exactly why
you are here," said the Conductor. "There
were a great many brothers who fought
against each other. And here, in this area, a
great battle will take place in which two
brothers will be at odds."

"The Battle of Chickamauga," Aly
said. "Dad has been telling us about it."

"Correct," he said, "the Battle of
Chickamauga."

"This will be our second time to go into a real war zone," I said with a shake of the head.

"Yes," said the Conductor, "and just as last time, the war is not your issue. Soldiers will fight and kill and die. You are not here to do their job, you are here to do yours. Your job concerns two brothers, George and Patrick Cape. Sixteen-year-old George has taken the Union side, and Patrick, two years his junior, holds fast to the Confederacy. Patrick is still at home in the large white farm house just across the way, and George is even now drilling with the Union forces just a few miles from here. The Battle of Chickamauga is just two days away, and much blood will be shed on these hills. It is your job to make sure that George and Patrick come through it alive. The devil is at work, and if someone does not intervene, they will meet each other personally in battle, and one or both of them will die. This cannot be allowed to happen. Both of them have been called to preach, and if they live, they will have sons and grandsons and even great-grandsons that preach as well, some of them right here in this area. The devil knows this, and he is seeking to use them to destroy each other before that can happen. If one kills the other, even the living brother will not survive to preach. The guilt will consume him, and many thousands will die and go to Hell as a result of the loss of these two young men. A concerned mother is at home right at this moment praying for them, in fact, she has been praying through the night. That is why you have been called, God is sending help in response to a mother's prayers."

"That sounds a lot like West Virginia," I said. "I just hope we can have the same success this time as then."

"We have to, Big Bro," Aly said. "We may want to kill you from time to time, but we sure can't let one of the Cape brothers actually, literally kill the other."

I cut my eyes at the little twerp, then turned back to the Conductor and said, "We'll get the job done or at least give it everything we've got in the effort. What should we do first?"

"You should have figured out by now that my job is merely to transport you to your assigned destination. What you do first is entirely up to you. But you should probably have asked what you should do second, because I know you well enough to know that the first thing you are going to do is pray."

He was right.

And we did.

Chapter Three

The area in and around Chickamauga is beautiful. As you drive down Battleground Parkway into Fort Oglethorpe, you can see the nearby mountains just a few short miles away, at least if you are in our time and not back in the past like we were at the moment. A few hours earlier we had driven past Bojangles and a Fitness Center and K-Mart and a Wendy's and a bunch more. But now all of that was gone, and all that remained were the rolling hills, meadows, and the lovely woodlands of Chickamauga. As the wagon bumped down a wooded trail, barely wide enough to fit through, I observed a beautiful mixture of oaks, maples, and pines. The air held the smell of cedar wood, and I could hear the birds chattering noisily to each other overhead. But it was the far off sound of massive amounts of men and horses and artillery moving about, a barely noticeable, buzzing, bustling noise that commanded my attention and made me cock my head to listen.

"They are eight miles away, in Chattanooga," the Conductor answered to the question I had not asked. "The valley acts as a sound funnel, bringing sound down off of the mountain. You are hearing General Rosecrans and the Army of the Cumberland, some one hundred thousand strong and in preparations. On the Confederate side, General Braxton Bragg and the Army of Tennessee are just a few miles from here making their plans. We have very little time to get you acclimated with the area and set on the right path to fulfill your mission."

"Where are we headed to right now?" Aly asked.

"It is time for you to begin to learn all you can about the Cape family. I will take you to the crossing of the Chickamauga Creek. Their farm house is a quarter of a mile on the other side of it. As always, please remember that you have till bedtime. Do what you can on this day, then find a safe place out of sight to go to sleep for the night, and when you do you will wake up back in the hotel, in your own time, as refreshed as if you had gotten a full night's sleep."

We knew the drill pretty well by now, so we rode on slowly in relative silence for a good little while. The bustling noises of the Army of the Cumberland were still humming in our ears and were joined by the creaking of leather and wood and metal as the donkey plodded on, pulling our wagon behind him. I began to wonder about the Cape family as we rode along. What had caused them to be divided on this issue? How is it that their beliefs on each side were so strong that two brothers were willing to fight and even kill each other over it?

"Wouldn't be the first time, Big Bro," said Aly. "Remember Cain and Abel?"

"What?" I said. "How did..."

"You were mumbling to yourself again," Carrie said with a smile. "You tend to do that when you are deep in thought. Deep, of course, being a relative term when it comes to your tiny brain."

"Seriously?" Aly snapped at her. "Is this really going to happen again? Do you two even have the ability to start a mission without slamming on each other first?"

"It's kind of like a mental stretching routine, Pipsqueak," I said with a smile. "And I don't mind Carrie trying to test me. Acolytes are like that with those they idolize."

"Aco what?" Aly said with a bewildered frown.

"Ooooooh, that's a big word for you, Big Brother," Carrie shot back. Then she turned to Aly and said, in her best professorial voice, "Acolyte: noun. Someone who follows and admires a leader." Then she smiled at her own intelligence and said, "But perhaps we should stick to the point. You wanted to know how the Cape family could become so divided. I suspect that our very first task will be to find out that vital piece of information. Once we know that, we may have a good start on getting them to not kill each other."

"That is an excellent plan, young lady," the Conductor said to us over his shoulder. "And you should be able to begin that quest right about...now," he said as he tugged on the reins and whoad the donkey and wagon to a stop.

"This is as far as I go for now. I need to stop right here inside the tree line; my Commander does not wish for me or my wagon to be seen. A hundred yards or so to the west of here you will find a small bridge that crosses the Chickamauga, Alexander Bridge. If you cross that bridge and then veer a bit to your right, you will come to a field of standing corn. You should be able to walk through that field, undetected, up to the back yard of the Cape family. From there you are on your own. Be careful, Night Heroes, and Godspeed.

A moment later the Conductor and our transportation drove off, back into the trees and out of sight.

"Well, Big Bro," Aly said with a wry smile, "This sure is better than last time. Instead of running for miles through the forests of Germany, we can jog a few hundred yards to the bridge, then head for the house just a quarter of a mile away. We will be positively lazy by the time this adventure is over!"

"Probably not, Squirt. If my memory is correct, the Chickamauga Battlefield is huge. We are definitely going to get our exercise in before this is all over. Let's get going."

And with that we began a slow jog to the bridge. When we arrived, we found an old wooden bridge across a wide, slow moving creek. The creek itself was bordered by a bunch of lovely Sourwood trees, with their bright red and orange fall leaves shining vibrantly from their slightly weeping branches. The water rippled peacefully as we crossed, utterly unconcerned with the wars and bloodshed in the world of men.

Having crossed the bridge, we soon came up on the cornfield. It was well over our heads and not much trouble at all to walk down the rows. And walk we did. As we made our way, I thought about the time in Matthew chapter twelve that Jesus and His disciples walked through a cornfield. On that day, their walk through the cornfield had caused problems. The Pharisees had seen

21

them eating some of that corn as they walked by. But that was not the problem; that was allowed under the law and expected by those familiar with the culture of the land. The problem was, they had not bothered to ceremonially wash their hands first. That "breach of decorum" had angered the Pharisees and made them fighting mad.

As I mused over that ridiculousness, a funny thought hit me, a thought I had never "thunk" before. I laughed out loud and said, "What were they doing in the corn field?"

"What?" both Carrie and Aly said at the same time.

"The Pharisees," I said. "What were the Pharisees doing in that corn field to begin with? They had money, and they were generally city boys. What were they doing in the corn field?"

"You're thinking of Matthew twelve, aren't you?" Carrie asked with a smile. Then, assuming she was correct, she answered the question I had just asked. "They were in that corn field for one reason: to pick a fight with Jesus. But we better keep our voices low, because anyone who realizes that we are here will probably want to pick a fight with us."

She was correct on both counts, naturally. So we fell silent once again and continued to walk. Soon we came to the end of the field, and instinctively we crouched down just inside the edge of it, wanting to see but not be seen.

One hundred feet or so away from the edge of the field, we saw a simple white farmhouse. A thin gray smoke was wafting upward out of the chimney, and the smell of some delicious home cooked meal was drifting to us on the breeze. The farmhouse was set up off of the ground on rock pilings, and we could see all the way under it and out the other side. Chickens were lazily pecking in the yard, and a hog pen to the far left of the yard was holding in a nice family of porkers who would undoubtedly be headed to market soon.

Behind the house was a two story barn, easily three times the size of the house. It had a hay loft, and we could hear horses whinnying in the stalls. The entire scene was like something out of a Norman Rockwell painting, which most adults my grandparents' age seem to have hanging somewhere around their house.

"Whadda ya think, Bro, what's our play?" asked Aly. I looked over at her, and she had a mischievous look on her face, clearly raring to go.

"Well, I'm thinking of the subtle route," I said. "Walking up to the door and knocking isn't a good idea, I think. We need to know more about what is going on before we make contact with the family."

"And how are we going to find out what is going on without making contact with them?" Carrie asked with a bit of a huff.

"Well, I'm thinking we should run, slide under the house, and eavesdrop," I said. I was only kidding of course, but I very quickly realized that my attempt at humor had been a very bad idea.

Aly was already out into the open, running for the house.

Chapter Four

We really had no choice, since we couldn't exactly let her go by herself. If anything happened to the runt I would never forgive myself. And if nothing happened to her, but we did not join her, she would never forgive me!

A split second later we were bolting after her. That kid is fast, really fast. But even with the head start, Carrie and I caught up to her about half way across the yard. A few seconds later we all dove headfirst up under the house and came to a sliding stop. We were fighting like crazy to control our breathing; we didn't want to be discovered. It would be awfully hard to explain what we were doing under the house.

Slowly, our breathing calmed, and the pounding in my head settled down. My heart, which had been racing, was finally getting back to a normal rhythm.

And then it skipped a beat, as the shout from above us made me jump and almost smack my head on a floor joist.

"It isn't acceptable; not at all! You have no right to dishonor our family and our father's memory!"

It was the voice of a young man, an angry young man. The voice that answered was every bit as angry, maybe more.

"Our father's memory is no excuse for wrongdoing! Nor is family, for that matter! This blight must be stopped; it is against the very Word of God."

"Our family is not involved in slavery, George; you know that. Our father worked the land with his own hands, and we worked it right beside him. Any help we had was hired help. How does taking up arms against your family, your friends, and your country, over a wrong that our family is not even involved in, fit into your view of Scripture? What about 'honor thy father and thy mother'? Have you forgotten that?"

"Our family is not involved, no," George snapped back at Patrick, "but this state, and indeed the Confederacy as a whole most certainly is. And if it means taking up arms, even against family and friends, then yes, I will do so. But I would rather not. I would rather both you and mother do the sensible thing: surrender the house and property, give yourselves up to General Rosecrans, and I will do what I can to make sure that the house and barn are not destroyed when the attack comes."

"We will do no such thing!" Patrick yelled at the top of his lungs. "Some of us still regard loyalty as a character trait of a Christian. Furthermore, our General Lee has no slaves, but your General Grant does. The hands of your northern friends are just as stained by the blight of slavery as the hands of any southerner. It is not right to solve this by war, especially not war against your own family."

"I do not wish to solve it by war; I wish for you and pig-headed people like you to solve it by laying down your arms. You cannot win this fight; the South cannot win this fight. You will be overrun, and Chickamauga will go down as the death knell of the Confederacy."

"You seem very sure of yourself, George, but perhaps you should not be. The Confederacy will win at Chickamauga, we will retake Chattanooga, and you will end up dead."

"Are you threatening me, Patrick? I can still whip you now just as soundly as I could when we were children; we do not need to wait until the battle is joined."

And on it went. The shouts grew louder, the threats more vehement. And then, as if a whistle had blown, they simply stopped. I strained to try and figure out why, and in just a few seconds, I knew.

Crying. The soft sobbing that could only come from the broken heart of a mother whose children are at homicidal odds.

We lay quietly for a good while, as the voices in the house softened to a murmur. We could not make out anymore what was being said, but we knew they were still talking. The minutes dragged into hours, and before long, the sun began to set.

"Ok, you two," I whispered, "we better slide out from under this house and make our way back into the trees, and go to sleep for our trip back home."

Slowly we began making our way toward the back of the house. We were within just a few feet when the unthinkable happened: the back door opened, and two sets of feet walked down the steps and stopped right at the bottom!

We froze.

We prayed not to be seen.

"Patrick," said the voice that we had come to know as George Cape, "please, for the sake of our mother, reconsider. I do not wish to kill you, nor do I wish our mother to die of a broken heart. Speak to her. Surrender the house; go someplace safe."

I did not want to be seen, but my curiosity was killing me. Ever so slowly I bent down and peered out from under the house, careful to stay just far enough back to avoid being seen, unless either of them bent down to see.

Both of the boys were tall for their age, easily a couple of inches taller than me. I was thicker than either of them though, more muscular by a good bit. I guessed that made us all about equal in weight, and with life-long farm work and being in the military, I judged that either of them would make for quite a fight if it ever came down to it.

George had short hair, black as a raven's wing, and deep brown eyes. His jaw was square, and his nose a bit large. Patrick, from behind, had hair only slightly lighter, but I could see the same square jaw as he turned a bit.

"George," he said, "my mind is set." Then with a heavy sigh and a shake of the head he said, "I regret that it has come to this."

"And I as well, my brother. But nothing is more important to me than this cause, nothing."

"Nor is anything more important to me than my home, our home," Patrick said softly but firmly.

"Then there is nothing left but battle, I suppose." It was George who said that, and I could hear a mixture of resolve and sadness in his voice as he did. Then he turned and walked away, and I could hear a mother begin to cry again as his brother walked back into the house.

With only moments left till nightfall, and not being able to run into the woods that George had just disappeared into, we crawled back up under the very middle of the house, and in mere moments we were all fast asleep.

Chapter Five

"What do you think went wrong?"

I could hear the words whispered into my ears, but it took a moment for my brain to register them and for me to respond. Finally I rolled over, sluggish, feeling like you do when you first wake up after a long night of sleep. That is always so weird, being active all night, going to sleep in the past, and waking up a split second later feeling like you've just slept all night and woke up,

"What do you mean?" I whispered back to Carrie. I could see the lumps in the other bed that I had come to identify as mom and dad. Their rythmatic breathing always made me feel good to hear. Those two are so much "one flesh" like the Bible describes, they even breathe alike when they sleep.

"Something had to go wrong somewhere along the way. Brothers don't fight and scream at each other like that when they both know the Lord. They are related by blood and by the blood of Jesus. Why are they intent on killing each other?"

Aly was still sleeping beside her, so I kept my voice low as I answered.

"They have forgotten that they have a higher calling."

"What?" Carrie asked as her forehead puckered.

"Both sides of the issue in the Civil War are, by themselves, worthy of fighting over. No one should own another human being, since every man is made in the image of God. Slavery was one of the biggest wrongs of all time. But no body of people should ever force another body of people to stay with them either. The North forcing the South to stay in the Union is a lot like a husband, bigger and stronger than a wife, dragging her back into the home when she tries to leave. If people do not want to stay, they should not be forced by violence to do so. But as big as both of those issues are, George and Patrick seem to have forgotten that they both have an even higher calling. Nothing is more important than preaching the gospel. Slaves need to hear it, masters need to hear it, presidents need to hear it, nations need to hear it. There is no higher calling than to be a preacher of the gospel. When people forget that, when they place the important above the essential, they end up trying to kill each other. That is what has gone wrong, and that is what we have to fix."

"Good speech, Bro," Aly said without opening her eyes.

"You little rat," I said with a smile, "how long have you been awake?"

"A few minutes. I had to wake up because of MY calling."

"Your calling?" Carrie asked with a confused look, "what exactly is your calling?"

"My stomach has called me to wake mom and dad up and have breakfast!" she said with a sunny smile.

"Tell your stomach to go back to sleep," said a gruff voice from the strongest man I know, my dad. That voice is always enough to make me stand up straight and do right, and now it made me almost jump out of my skin! How much had he heard of our conversation?

Apparently nothing. If he did, he never mentioned it.

An hour later we were all showered, dressed, and down in the hotel lobby for a continental breakfast. Dad browsed the paper while scarfing down a whole-grain bagel, mom sipped her coffee, and the girls and I had a "delicious and nutritious" breakfast of donuts and honey buns.

A few minutes later, after washing all of the sticky off, we were in the Yukon and heading down to the church.

Lots of churches were in attendance, even in the morning service. A whole group was there from Kings Mountain, just on the other side of the county from our home church. They were from Love Valley. Their youth choir sang, and man, did they light it up! There is a really cool song they sing, "I'm Not Going to Hell." I love that song, mostly because I know that I myself am definitely not going to Hell! I got saved a few years ago, and I get to go to Heaven when I die.

Joe Arthur preached first. I love Brother Arthur. He is funny, but is also very encouraging. He is one of those preachers that, as my dad says, "isn't going to hurt you."

Brother Sammy Allen preached next. He is getting older, and his mind wanders quite a bit now, but he still has what is important: a touch of God on him. I've never seen him preach without the altars being filled. His prayer life powers his preaching, he is known to pray every single day for hours and hours at a time.

Soon it was time for lunch. The fellowship hall was so packed that there was no way we could all fit in, so me and the girls and a bunch of the other kids went outside to eat, and then took some time to play and make friends.

After a while we heard the music start, and that was our cue to head back into the service. Brother Eric Brown and a couple of others preached, and it was all really good. Brother Brown used an awesome illustration about Jesus washing the feet of His disciples. There was not a dry eye in the house by the time he was done.

Supper time came and went, we were all full again, and then it was back in for the evening service. Dad preached one of his favorite messages, "Choosing Your Final Destination." Several more people got saved, and most everyone spent a good long time around the altar. I loooooooove services like that!

Finally we were finished, and it was back to the hotel. It took us maybe forty-five minutes to get ready for bed, five minutes for me and dad, forty for mom and the girls. Then mom and dad prayed with us, threatened our lives if we talked or giggled after lights out, and turned the lights off. I lay there for a few minutes, praying, thanking God for the day, and for the ones who came to know Christ as their Savior. Then, little by little, I drifted off to sleep.

Chapter Six

As usual, our sleep was short lived. We all awoke to the sounds of wheels creaking and rolling and the feeling of bouncing around in the back of the wagon. I sat up, and Carrie and Aly did the same beside me.

"Good morning, Night Heroes, I trust the service went well last night. Are you ready to begin your second day of the mission?"

"Yes, sir!" we all chimed in unison.

"Good. Then where would you like to begin?"

"Well, sir," I said slowly, "I am thinking that we are going to have to find some way to mediate a conversation between George and Patrick and get them to remember what is really important. If that doesn't work, we will have to find some way to get one or the other of them out of the way until the battle is over. That second option would be awfully difficult, so I would much prefer the first."

I saw both the Conductor and my sisters nodding their heads at my reasoning, so I continued.

"What about the direct approach? We don't want to break any rules, so I guess what I am asking is, would it be acceptable for us to go to the house, knock on the door, introduce ourselves as preacher's kids and ask to speak to Patrick? We don't have to tell them that we are not from their time. We just have to find a way to convince them to trust us enough to talk to them."

"Well, I suppose that is one way," said the Conductor, "and there are no rules against it, as long as you do not give any indication of your true time or how you got here. So if that is the direction you want to pursue, you may do so."

And so it was that a little while later we were once again crossing the Chickamauga via the Alexander Bridge. We walked through the cornfield as before, and each step through it made my chest tighten up just a bit more. I actually liked running and fighting and scheming and things like that much more than sitting down to talk. Just thinking of how I was going to explain our presence here made me nervous.

When we got to the edge of the cornfield, we peered out and saw that everything looked much like it had the day before. Same chickens pecking in the yard, same pigs rooting around in the pen, same smoke drifting out of the chimney. We watched it all in contemplative silence for a few minutes, then without a word, we bowed our heads to pray.

One by one, a few minutes later, we lifted our heads, and I began to speak.

"Ok, guys, here's the plan. We walk up to the door, knock on it, and hopefully get invited in. The gist of our conversation needs to be that we are preacher's kids, and that we heard that there were a couple of young preachers in the house. We want to talk to them and ask them about the ministry."

"Got it," they both answered, and immediately we were up and walking toward the door.

A lot of times we Christians go on what is called "Soul winning," or "Door-knocking visitation." It basically involves knocking on the door of perfect strangers, introducing yourselves, and talking to them about the Lord. We kids have all done that with our folks since we were babies in carriers, so this was nothing new to us. But this was going to be a horse of a different color. Knocking on a door that was a century and a half or so before our time to try and keep brothers from killing each other? Wild, very wild...

The noise of the knock on the door almost made me jump a little, and I was the one doing the knocking! The old oak door was solid and had a strong sound to it. Presently, we heard the sound of footsteps walking gently through the house and to the door. The floor creaked as the steps got nearer.

Finally, the door opened, and we were eye to eye with a plain, yet somehow pretty face. It was care-worn, and the bags under her eyes told us that she had spent many recent nights in prayer but very few in sleep.

"Yes, may I help you, children?"

The voice had a soft southern drawl to it. My dad says that is the way people talk in Heaven. As proof, he says, "Ask yourself one question. Do you believe the angels in Heaven say (and here he puts on a thick Brooklyn accent) 'Whadda ya wahnt? Cahfee?' or do you think they say (in his best Georgia drawl) 'Hay theyah, Sugah, would yew like sum cawfee?"

My mind wandered for just a second as I thought of that, but it snapped back to attention as I felt Carrie elbow me.

"Uh, yes, ma'am, you surely can," I said. "We are the Warner kids, and we heard that your boys have been called to preach. Would it be possible for us to speak with them?"

She got a faint smile on her face at that, a smile mixed with a tinge of sadness. Then she opened the door wide and said, "Come right in, children, come in and have a seat at my table."

The inside of the old white farm house was an interesting study. The table and chairs were clearly homemade, sturdy yet plain. The old white tablecloth looked like it was hand knitted by some family matriarch. It was a bit torn and tattered, but was as clean and white as the wind-driven snow. A single window looked out to the east, positioned perfectly to catch the rays of each day's rising sun. There was a staircase to the left of the kitchen area that I guessed led upstairs to the bedrooms. By that staircase there was an old rocking chair, and beside that chair a small table with a large old Bible on it. I figured that this dear lady had spent many an hour in that chair, reading that old Bible.

We sat down at the table, and the lady began to talk to us as she bustled about the kitchen. She was pulling glasses out of the cabinets as she bustled and talked, and soon was pouring the contents of a pitcher into the glasses. Soon there were three glasses sitting in front of us, each one filled with cool milk that I guessed had been milked from cows in the barn just a little while ago.

"So, Warner children, is it? Tell me, where are you from, and what brings you out to my farm?"

"Well ma'am," I began as politely as I could, "as I said, we are wanting to talk to your sons, if we may. We are preacher's kids ourselves, and we heard that your boys had been called to preach. We just wanted to talk to them about that if we could."

"I see," she said. Then she continued, "Where are you from? I do not know of the name Warner in any of these parts."

I tensed up a bit, but tried my best not to show it. How was I going to answer that? Finally I smiled as I realized that honesty was actually the best policy in this.

"We're from North Carolina," I said, "from a little town called Mooresboro. Not many folks have ever heard of it."

I was guessing that like most folks in those days, she had probably never been out of her own state and would not know much about other states, and therefore would not ask many questions. Boy, was I wrong on that one!

"North Carolina? Why, that's my home state! How far away and what direction is Mooresboro from Raleigh?"

Uh oh, I was in trouble already! Fortunately, my big brained sister stepped in.

I am sure that under normal circumstances she would have love to have seen me squirm, but right now we had a job to do, and I was doing very poorly at it.

"Oh, Mooresboro is a couple of hundred miles to the west of Raleigh," Carrie said with a sugary smile. "An evangelistic meeting with our father brought us down this way, and as we began to get to know folks around here, we heard about your sons."

And then the unthinkable happened:

"Well, if you are preacher's kids, why aren't you asking your own father about the ministry?"

Chapter Seven

We were stunned. The smile on Mrs. Cape's face was gone, and she looked as stern as a middle school principle dealing with misbehaving children. Clearly we had underestimated her!

"I am not trying to be harsh, children," she continued, "but you may have heard that there is a war raging all around us. No one knows who can be trusted and who cannot. And in the midst of all of that, three unknown youngsters show up at my door to ask about my sons, both of whom are in the service. So I will ask again, why aren't you asking your own father about this?"

The silence was deafening, and as heavy as the thick fog on the mountains. I knew without asking that both Carrie and Aly were doing exactly what I was doing, praying like crazy.

You know, it's funny: in desperate times, answers to prayer seem to come quick, and in almost miraculous fashion. It did this time, to sweet little Aly, who had not yet spoken.

"Ma'am, we can't ask our father. He isn't living now," she said, and then she began to cry.

Genius! Sheer genius! She was telling the absolute truth! Dad wasn't living now, and he wouldn't be for over a hundred more years! The tears were just a nice acting job, a really good touch.

Maybe it was the fact that this lady herself was a widow raising sons without a father, but it worked like a charm.

"Oh, sweetheart, I am so sorry," she cooed as she rushed to Aly's side and put motherly arms around her. "I didn't mean to hurt you. I understand now. Your father came down here for a meeting and passed away. You did right to come looking for God's people for help. That's what Christians do."

Mrs. Cape cooed and soothed and mothered us all for the next little while. I felt bad for her feeling bad, since we would go to sleep in a few hours and wake up to see our dad, but we had, in fact, been honest in everything we said. And if we didn't succeed in our mission, she would have a much bigger reason to be sad!

After a while, Mrs. Cape began to talk to us about her sons. Part of it we groaned inside at, the part about the boys fighting on opposite sides. Part of it we really enjoyed hearing; how they were raised, when they got saved, the day they both got called to preach. But it didn't take long for me to grimace and stop enjoying any of it. I stopped enjoying it the moment she said, "But neither of the boys are here right now. George is already in Chattanooga with the Union army, and Patrick left late last night to meet back up with General Bragg and the Army of Tennessee. They are right now gathering near the Brotherton house over by Snodgrass Hill. But you can still talk to him, if you hurry. You obviously know your way around these parts pretty well, so just head over that direction, and you should be able to get someone to point him out to you. Hurry, children, and be careful. Everyone is trigger happy right now, and if you are not careful you will find yourselves being shot at from both sides!"

A moment later we were out of the house, back into the cornfield, and then back into the woods. Then we stopped, looked at each other, and in unison said, "Where in the world is Snodgrass Hill?"

You know, in our grandparent's day, we would have looked at a map purchased at a gas station. In our parent's day we would have reached for an atlas of the United States. In our day we would have punched the address into a GPS. But at the moment, not a one of those options were available to us!

"We have a problem, Twerps," I said. "According to the Conductor," the battle of Chickamauga should start tomorrow. The Confederates may be nearby there now, but by tomorrow night, General Thomas and the Union forces will be holding Snodgrass Hill. We have little to no time, but we also have no idea in the world how to find the Brotherton House, or Snodgrass Hill, or Patrick or George Cape."

"No, but by tomorrow we will," Aly said with a smile. And then in answer to the quizzical looks on my face and Carrie's, she said, "Last night I overheard dad telling mom that there are no afternoon services tomorrow, and that he is going to take us out to the Chickamauga Battlefield for the day. By tomorrow night we should know our way around really well."

"But by tomorrow night the battle will have already started!" Carrie moaned.

"Well, do either of you have a better idea? I mean, if you want to go poking around the woods in a Civil War zone asking where General Bragg and the Confederate forces are..."

As Aly's words trailed off, we knew. She was right, and there was not one thing we could do until day three. We all went a little deeper into the woods and spent the last few hours of daylight doing my least favorite thing, being still and quite. Then as night fell, with my stomach in knots over a very unproductive day, I fell into a fitful sleep.

Chapter Eight

As rays of light began to sneak in under the thick curtain at the Super 8, I blinked a few times, yawned, and stretched. Mom was already up, ironing our dress clothes. It didn't take long for all of the rest of us to be up as well. The girls always got access to the shower first, and then dad and I took our showers, longing for the day when there would actually be some hot water for us too!

Soon we were dressed and down in the lobby eating breakfast. The nice folks behind the counter were checking new folks in, cars were passing back and forth outside, and a few moments later a church bus from Hiawassee, Georgia, left the parking lot. I knew that meant that it was about time for us to go, and sure enough, I heard dad say, "Load up, Warner kids, time to go."

As the scenery passed by the windows of our Yukon, I envisioned it as we were seeing it at night, with all of the businesses and new buildings gone. But soon all my time for musing was gone, as we pulled into the parking lot of Bible Baptist. We gathered our Bibles, the girls grabbed their mini suitcases (my name for their purses), and we headed inside. We could already hear the beautiful sounds of stringed instruments: guitars, mandolins, and banjos. This time it was Pastor Chris Simpson and a couple of others playing the prelude.

The song leader called us to order, we sang a couple of congregational numbers, and then it was time for the preaching to begin. We heard from Evangelist John Morgan, a great old man named Stinnett Ballew, and the morning was closed out by Pastor Barry Philbeck. They all did a really great job telling about Jesus and explaining the Bible. I tell you, being a Christian is the life!

The pastor announced for those who had not yet heard that there would be lunch in the fellowship hall, but no afternoon services. The evening services would start back at seven o'clock.

We ate lunch, we laughed and talked with our friends, and then before we knew it we were back in the Yukon heading for the hotel. We changed out of our dress clothes into some every day wear and headed right back to the vehicle to go tour the Chickamauga Battlefield. Dad was excitedly telling us all how much we were going to enjoy this new experience. If he only knew that we had already been there, twice, the last two nights, a hundred and fifty years ago or so! Wow...

As we drove into the battlefield park, though, I was surprised to find out how much I was surprised! The land was the same, but everything else was very different. For starters, there were big monuments everywhere, and I mean everywhere. The battlefield parks that we were used to, like the Kings Mountain Battlefield back home, had maybe a dozen or so monuments in the whole place. In Chickamauga there are literally thousands of them! Some are shaped like soldiers, some like cannons, some are just large plaques with writing on them, and a good many are actually giant concrete acorns!

We pulled into the welcome center and went inside. There were displays to see and also a short video presentation about the battle. I knew that Carrie and Aly were doing the same thing that I was: praying that dad would want to see it. That could give us some vital intel on what we were dealing with.

We really didn't need to worry too much, dad is drawn to things like that like a moth to a flame.

The video was really well done as far as how it looked. It was though, I thought, a bit one sided, making the North out to be completely in the right. But it did give us exactly what we were hoping for, a really good overview of the battlefield area, and an understanding of where troops would be...are you ready for this...tonight once we fell asleep. Wild, just wild.

Once the video was done we headed back to the vehicle. We had learned that Chickamauga is not a walking thing, it is a driving thing.

"The park is massive," dad said over his right shoulder. "There's no way you could cover it all by walking, it would take months for that."

I cut my eyes over at the girls, and they just grinned.

The tour of Chickamauga has numbers to follow, but really it is almost impossible to do so. There are crossroads coming off of the main rode, and then crossroads coming off of all of the cross roads! I could see dad getting a bit frustrated with trying to follow the numbers in order, so soon he just started "putting his nose into the wind and sniffing for interestingness," as he put it.

That turned out to be a help to us.

After a few twists and turns, Carrie and Aly and I almost in unison clapped our hands over our mouths to keep from shouting in surprise. Right there in front of us was Alexander Bridge! It was a newer version, made of concrete, but it was in the exact same spot as the old wooden one we had been crossing over each night! The trees looked much the same, the water was the same, the curve of the land was the same.

"Let's get out and take a look," we heard dad say as he pulled the Yukon off onto the side of the road. A minute later we were all out onto the bridge, listening to the river ripple peacefully by.

We all stood there silently for a moment, and then mom said, "It's amazing, really. You kids probably don't understand how significant this spot is, and all of the history that you are right in the middle of."

It is very, very hard not to laugh at a moment like that.

But, since laughter at that moment would be hard to explain, we held it back.

After a while dad got us all back into the vehicle, and we started exploring again. We crossed over the bridge, drove maybe a half mile or so, and then dad decided to turn left onto Viniard Road. We drove past one section of forest after another, all of them dotted with monument after monument. After maybe a mile and a half or so we came to a stop sign. Dad was in high gear, relishing the chance to guess right or left at random, and see what there was to see. He chose to turn right, and away we went on LaFayette Road. After a minute or two, dad stopped again. There was an old looking cabin up in the trees and a marker nearby.

We all piled out of the vehicle and started walking. We very quickly came up on a marker, and what we read on it made me gasp, and realize again how very good our God is! Out of all the hundreds of places we could have ended up in the battlefield, the marker told us that we had come to the one place we really needed to find. The marker read:

"War Comes to the Brothertons"

The great battle raged around this family farm.

"At the time of the battle of Chickamauga, George and Mary Brotherton and their children lived in a log house here. In the surrounding fields they grazed cattle and grew corn and hay. To escape the battle, some of the Brothertons and other local families took refuge in a ravine about a mile from here. There they endured hunger and cold, and prayed for their boys serving in the Confederate army.

Tom Brotherton, one of the sons, played a key role in the battle. Because Tom 'knew every pig trail through these woods,' General Longstreet, commander of the Confederate left wing, employed him as a scout. Tom served with pride, telling his brother Jim, 'It's a sorry lad that won't fight for his own home.' Jim Brotherton also fought for the South.

We stood there looking at the marker for a minute, and then mom and dad went ahead a little ways to check out the cabin. When they did, I whispered to Carrie and Aly:

"Check it out, guys, look where we are! This tells us what we knew we needed to know, and even what we didn't know that we needed to know."

"What on earth is that supposed to mean?" Carrie asked with a bit of irritation at my last sentence. She like things to be understandable, and sometimes I have a bit of trouble with that.

"It means," I said slowly, "that not only do we now know how to get to the Brotherton house where we can find Patrick, but we also now know that there is a way to do so that may keep us from getting shot. If we can find that ravine, we can use it to keep us under cover until we are very near to the house"

"Ahhh, now that makes sense," Carrie said softly, while brushing her hair away from her face. The wind was picking up a bit, and the girls were struggling with their hair. Just one more reason I like being a guy.

We followed mom and dad up to the cabin, looked around a while, and then headed back for the Yukon. Dad said that he had a surprise for us, and that we would have to come back and see the rest of the battlefield another day.

And what a surprise! I was a little bit disappointed when we first started driving out of the battlefield and toward the big city of Chattanooga. But pretty soon I was glad that we had. After weaving up some winding mountain roads, we ended up at Ruby Falls! I had heard of it, but this was my first time ever seeing it. Friends, if you are ever within a hundred miles of Chattanooga, be sure to and go and see Ruby Falls.

We started the tour by going down an elevator, way down into the heart of the mountain. Then the tour guide took us on a nice long hike through a massive system of underground caves. It had been discovered on December 30, 1928, by accident. There were amazing rock formations all along the way, but at the very end, more than a thousand feet underground, was a massive waterfall! You expect to see waterfalls on top of mountains, but not underneath them! It was absolutely breathtaking.

We stood there in awe of it for a while, took a bunch of pictures, and then the guide led us back to the elevator. A few minutes later we were back out through the gift shop and on the front porch once more. It was then that I heard my dad say, "Kids, come check this out. This is something that people seem to be afraid to say anymore, in this day when the stupidity of evolution is now accepted as fact, but this guy was right. Read this."

And we did. The "this" we read was a brass plaque with the likeness of Leo Lambert, the man that had first discovered the falls. The plaque read:

> "Discovering Ruby Falls was like discovering God. At first it is very dark, scary and uncertain. You don't know what lies ahead.

> "You bump into things you didn't even realize were there

and you suffer injuries bumps and bruises. You fall down into sticky, sticky mud and mire and feel like you cannot go on. But you get up with a feeling that somewhere ahead lies something more wonderful than you could ever imagine.

"As you add light to what you discovered you find that the things that caused you suffering and injury were wonderful, God made things, put there for you to witness and give you joy. It is all more than you ever imagined you could witness. It is God, and Ruby Falls and the Lookout Mountain Cave are God's creations, made for man to enjoy."

"Remember that," dad said. "Things this wonderful did not happen by accident. God made them, all of them. I expect you to be explorers, discoverers, students of the creation that God has made. Know the subject well enough to be able to help those that have fallen victim to the idiocy of evolution."

Ruby Falls had been a blast, but our time for daytime adventure was pretty much over. We had to get back to the hotel to get cleaned up for supper and service. After seeing Ruby Falls, I was looking forward to getting to church and personally telling the Lord thank you for all the wonderful things He has made! I know I can do that anywhere, but somehow it always feels a little better to do it in His house.

We got back to the hotel, got cleaned up, and went to the church for supper. Then it was on into the auditorium, where the sweetest singing and instrument playing you could imagine was already starting. It didn't take long for the place to fill up, and the atmosphere was just electric.

As great as the singing was, it didn't hold a candle to the preaching. My dad preached a cool message on Adam, "Adam Knew What He Was Doing." Then Pastor Philbeck preached a really encouraging message called "I've Been Bitten, But I Ain't Quittin!" I love messages like that, they make me realize that the best thing I can do is just serve the Lord no matter what.

After a really good altar call, we dragged our tired and happy selves back to the Yukon and went back to the hotel. We prayed together as a family, and within minutes we were sound asleep, and then wide awake.

Chapter Nine

The sun filtering through the trees is not what woke me up this time. The smell of gunpowder, the heavy thudding of the cannons, the clashing of swords, all of that worked together to jolt me out of a sound sleep. We were in the back of the wagon, hidden back in some trees. I quickly looked around and took stock of the situation. Carrie and Aly were there beside me. The Conductor was hunkered down in the floorboard of the wagon, looking around warily. I could not see any soldiers or armies nearby us in the woods, but I knew that that didn't prove they weren't there. There could well be soldiers hidden very near to us, so we were going to have to be very, very careful.

"Welcome back, Night Heroes." I do hope you learned a great deal yesterday, and are ready to put it into action. As you can hear, the battle has begun. These forests are now filled with nearly 200,000 men, and they are intent on killing whomever gets in their way. George and Patrick are now at extreme risk. Hold on tight, I am going to make our way back toward the bridge. The Master has secured one spot for us near the bridge that I will be able to take you to, with no one bothering us. After that, you will be in danger every step you take."

With a quiet "Giddap!" and a slap of the reins, the donkey started pulling the wagon again. We weaved through gullies, around knolls, under low hanging tree boughs, and finally came to our spot near the bridge. We were covered in pine needles, sap, and bark from all of the branches we had been dragged under.

"My apologies for the rough ride," the Conductor said, "but it was necessary to get you here without being seen."

"No problem, you did a great job," I answered back, and then a moment later he was fading off into the trees, leaving us to our work.

"Ok, Big Bro, what now?" Aly asked.

"In general, we head slightly northwest. I say 'in general' because I suspect that we may have to alter our path based on silly little things like bullets and cannonballs! If we can get anywhere near the Brotherton

House, my plan is for us to make a wide circle around it, looking for the ravine. Once we find that, we take it as near as it comes to the house, then we come out in the open and look for Patrick."

That brought an unbelieving shake of the head from Carrie.

"Uhh, and how exactly do you plan on introducing us? 'Hi, we're the Night Heroes, we traveled back through time, and we want to keep one of your soldiers from killing one of the enemy soldiers?' "

"Honestly, I haven't thought that far in advance," I said. "Why don't we see if we can avoid getting shot first, and then worry about that later?"

Yes, she (Carrie) did it. Again.

"Waaaay to go big brother, great plan. Names come to mind at this point. Not names like Macarthur or Pershing or Roosevelt, mind you, more like Goofy and Donald and Daffy."

"Ok, Pipsqueak, I know you've just been waiting to use that on me again, ever since West Virginia," I said. "But do you have a better idea?"

"Nope, I absolutely do not," she said with a giggle, "I just enjoy the way all of that sounds rolling off of my lips!"

"Great. Just great. Then why don't we get started, and if you think of any genius plan along the way, just let me know."

Running through the forest is nothing new to us. We got a lot of experience in that during our World War II adventure in Germany. But then there had been very few troops to worry about, and a very big area to move around in. Now we would have to watch for a couple hundred thousand people, all in a much smaller area.

We crossed the bridge and started off toward the north west at a trot. The air was already thick with the acrid smell of gunpowder. We made the first few hundred yards with no problem, and I was beginning to feel really good about our chances. I should have known better.

"Halt! Who goes there?"

The voice was an angry shout, but an anger mixed with a tinge of fear.

I froze.

I'm glad Carrie didn't.

She grabbed Aly by the hand and bolted past me like a scared rabbit, and instantly I joined them. Bullets came whizzing past us, snapping tree branches, and leaving angry scars on the trunks of trees that were just inches from us.

I didn't have any idea which side it was that was shooting at us, and I really didn't care. A bullet is a rather impersonal thing, and whether it is fired by friend or foe is irrelevant when it is being fired at you!

We ran like track stars, blazing through thickets and swatting aside the low hanging boughs of any trees that happened to get in our way.

Just when I thought we were in the clear, bark exploded off of a tree right beside me, stinging the right side of my face. I grabbed the girls and swerved right, judging that the bullet must have come from the left of me. We were now running without any sense of which direction we were going. If this kept up, we were as likely to end up in Chattanooga as we were to end up at the Brotherton house! I was in utter panic, knowing that now not only were George and Patrick Cape at risk of losing their lives, but we were too.

I don't know how, but in the midst of all of the chaos and frantic running for our lives, God brought a Bible passage to my mind. It is in the book of Acts, where Paul and the other missionaries were trying to go one direction, and it just wouldn't work out. It says, "Now when they had gone throughout Phrygia and the region of Galatia, and were forbidden of the Holy Ghost to preach the word in Asia, after they were come to Mysia, they assayed to go into Bithynia: but the Spirit suffered them not."

"Where are we?!?" Carrie screamed as we ran.

"I don't know, just keep bypassing the closed doors, and running for the open ones!" I shouted in return.

Neither of them answered me, they just kept running. I knew that they knew their Bibles well enough to know what I was thinking. God sent us here to do this mission, and we were just going to have to trust that every bullet that hit a tree was His way of saying, "No, I forbid you to go that way, go this way!"

We ran, oh did we run.

And then the ground under our feet simply disappeared.

Chapter Ten

The last time we went falling through the sky, we were wearing parachutes. Sadly, not this time.

Since I was in front, I landed first, and then tumbled farther and farther down till I hit bottom. Then Carrie landed on me. Then Aly landed on both of us. We were under some kind of a bush, and I was pretty sure that every bone in my body was broken. I did not have any air in my lungs, I lost all of that when Carrie landed on me. I guess that is why she was able to say it before I did:

"I think we found the ravine."

"Uh, yeah," I grunted as I got a little bit of air into my lungs, "I would say probably so."

And then from Aly, "That...was...AWESOME!"

I just giggled and shook my head. "You wouldn't be saying that if you were the one on the bottom of the pile, Pipsqueak. Now how about you two removing yourselves from my rib cage?"

Slowly and painfully we extricated ourselves from the bush and from each other. We stood up, brushed ourselves off, checked for broken bones, and thankfully seemed to have none.

"Well, we're no worse for wear," I said, and then I started laughing, mostly out of relief.

Now, the thing about laughing is, it is usually very contagious. Especially with the three of us. When one of us starts laughing, it usually jumps off onto the other two and gets them laughing as well. But for some reason, Carrie and Aly weren't laughing with me. In fact, both of them had gotten very serious and very still. And did I mention pale? They were both suddenly very pale too.

That's about when the hair on my neck started to rise a little bit, and I got this ominous feeling that I was being watched. I turned around, very slowly, looked up on the far edge of the ravine...

and stared into the very wicked looking barrel of an old style rifle. It was being held by a young man that appeared to be not much older than myself, maybe a touch taller, but with a care-worn face that would have been much better suited for a sixty year old. He was wearing grey trousers, a tan, home-made looking top, and had a powder horn hanging from a leather belt on his side. Behind him were ten or twelve other men, some older, some younger, all with the same grey pants, and all with different kinds of homemade looking shirts or jackets.

I gulped, hard, and raised my hands slowly. I could tell by the shadows on the ground that Carrie and Aly behind me were doing the exact same thing.

"If it weren't for the little girls behind you, I'd shoot you where you stand, Yankee," the rifle carrier said with an angry drawl. I felt my ears getting red with anger at being called a Yankee, but I suspected Carrie and Aly were even madder still over being called little girls. If I didn't do something quick, one of those two would come up out of the gully after that guy, and things would get ugly, very, very ugly. Fortunately, anyone who has been around a Bible for a while knows just the way to go in a situation like this. Proverbs 15:1 says, "A soft answer turneth away wrath: but grievous words stir up anger." This was definitely not the time to go stirring up anger, especially since we were on the wrong end of that gun!

So when I answered, it was in a very soft, kind voice, "I'm not a Yankee, sir, none of us are. My sisters and I are from North

Carolina. I'm looking for a man in your unit, Patrick Cape. Could you please take us to him and allow us to speak to him? His mother said he was with the troops near the Brotherton's house."

"Don't know no Patrick Cape," the rifleman said, "what I do know is that General Longstreet is going to want to talk to you, before you get to talk to anybody else. Yanks are pretty low, wouldn't be a bit surprised if they were using kids as spies now. Get up here, slowly, and don't try anything dumb if you want to live to see nightfall."

Oh boy, did we ever want to see nightfall!

Chapter Eleven

Lieutenant General James Longstreet did not seem like a happy type of a man. As he sat in his seat behind the table, looking at me and my sisters like we were as evil as the devil himself, I couldn't help but smile (on the inside, friend, only on the inside) just a little at one thought. This man was going to try and learn everything he possibly could about us; but I already knew a great deal about him.

He shifted in his seat a bit, mumbling from behind a bushy black beard that spilled eight or ten inches down his chest. He had a high forehead, and black hair slicked over to one side, beady eyes, and huge bags underneath them. I knew from history class, and from our research yesterday, that he had only recently arrived in the area along with 12,000 of his men from the army of Northern

Virginia. He was ill-tempered at the delay that caused him to arrive so shortly before the battle, and now he seemed even more ill-tempered at having to deal with "three Yank spies," as his men were calling us.

It was clear that if he had only been looking at me, he would have believed the story instantly. But seeing my two sisters with me, (who, by the way, were acting positively angelic. Award winning performance, that.) he seemed to not be so sure. He looked at us, then around the walls of the tent, then back to us yet again.

"Now then, why don't you tell me once again why you are here, and who it is that you so badly desire to speak to?"

His voice was a bit nasally, very tense, and incredibly condescending. I had already answered that same set of questions for him at least three times, but, having little choice, I did so again.

"As I said, sir, we are here to speak to Patrick Cape. He is a young soldier under your command. We aren't trying to interfere with the battle in any way. I know this is incredibly bad timing, but my need to speak with him is of a much more important nature than anything about the war. It is about the Lord; it is about the ministry. He doesn't know me, but I heard that he has been called to preach, and I need to speak to him about that."

The approach I was taking was a long shot, and I knew it. My hope was that, since most people north or south in the eighteen hundreds were first and foremost very religious people, maybe this man would actually believe anything related to God or the ministry was actually important enough for him to pull one simple soldier in and let me speak to him. I wasn't trying to stop an entire army, I just needed a few minutes with one young man.

Longstreet looked at me silently for a least a minute or two without saying a word. During that moment of silence, a thought occurred to me. Sadly, it was of a decidedly non-helpful nature. The thought that popped into my head was, *I wonder if this man would give me his autograph? It would be pretty cool to have an autograph from a civil war general that I actually met in person!*

I quickly stuffed that bad idea down into the wastebasket of my weird little mind.

"You want me to pull a soldier away from his defensive position, when we are even now trying to keep the gloved hand of the north from crushing the bare throat of the south?"

I gulped a little, sensing that things might not be going well.

"And you expect me to believe that you brought your two sisters onto the battlefield with you for that purpose, and no other?"

I opened my mouth to answer, but never got the chance. The table nearly shattered under the force of his fist as he slammed it down and shouted, "Spies! You are spies, and you are going to pay the price for that crime! Guards!"

As he shouted for them, and they came running in from outside, I could feel my world beginning to spin like a top. Things were going badly, very, very badly.

"Take these girls to the cook wagon. They will be our 'guests' for the remainder of the war. They will no doubt be very useful at peeling potatoes and preparing meals for the men."

"Yes, sir!" the guard answered with a snap salute. "And what of the boy?"

Longstreet smiled, no really it was more like he sneered as he said the words. "For now, put him in the makeshift supply shed and lock him up tight. Tonight, once the battle has ended for the day, we will make an example of him in the most vivid way possible."

"Sir?" the soldier questioned.

It was then the general said the two most frightening words I think I have ever heard. He looked at the guard and very simply said, "Hang him."

Chapter Twelve

I lay on my back in the cool dirt of the supply shed. There was no light within, but a crack in the boards about two-thirds of the way up on the western side was letting in a few rays of the fast fading sun.

It had been quite a sight in that tent when Longstreet said what he did about hanging me. Carrie and Aly had gone ballistic, and it had taken four men to keep them away from Longstreet! One of those men, poor guy, was going to be singing soprano for a very long time. When Carrie kicks, she kicks very hard, and very accurately!

I finally got them calmed down, I had to, or they would have ended up hanging with me. Besides, a smart person picks his time to act, and that was definitely not the right time.

Once we were out of sight and (hopefully) out of mind, then maybe we could figure a way out of this mess.

I was not calm on the inside, not by any means, but I was forcing myself to keep my emotions under control. I knew we were in a mess, a bad one. The way things were going, George or Patrick or both would end up shot, I would end up hanged, Carrie and Aly would end up prisoners for life, and mom and dad would wake up to three empty beds in the hotel room! We knew from the Conductor's careful warnings that, if we were held prisoner anywhere when night came, we would not get to go home that night, we would be stuck. We had only a few hours to get out of this, or else!

Thinking while laying on my back was not helping any, so I got up and paced back and forth in the darkness. By counting my steps I realized that I could take exactly twelve steps from front to back. "Twelve steps, turn. Twelve steps, turn. Twelve steps, turn. Twelve steps, turn," I was mumbling to myself. Then I started playing with the words. "A dozen, twelve, a dozen. A dozen, twelve, noon is twelve too."

It was silly, but for some reason it just felt like I ought to keep doing it.

"A dozen, twelve, a dozen. A dozen, twelve, noon is twelve, and so is midnight."

Midnight? Now why did that word seem to mean so much to my heart right then?

My mind was racing, something felt...familiar. Think! Think! What am I feeling?

And then I knew. I was feeling what I had felt many times since accepting Christ as my savior, I was feeling what my dad calls "the urging of the Spirit." There was something about midnight that God was heavily trying to draw my attention to. Midnight... midnight...

And then it hit me. As usual, it was a passage from the Bible. This time it was Acts 16:25-26, which I knew said, "And at midnight Paul and Silas prayed, and sang praises unto God: and the prisoners heard them. And suddenly there was a great earthquake, so that the foundations of the prison were shaken: and immediately all the doors were opened, and every one's bands were loosed."

I knew those were the words the Lord wanted me to hear, but why? Did He seriously expect me to sing right now? I mean, really, that couldn't be it. Could it? Oh, man, I was about to make myself look like a mental patient...

I started low.

"God is so gooooood, God is so gooooood, God is so gooooood He's so good to me..."

The urging in my heart seemed to say "Louder! I am worth more volume than that, sing louder!"

And so I did.

"He answers prayer... He answers prayer.... He answers prayer, He's so good to me..."

But the urging in my heart still didn't seem to be satisfied, so I kicked it up another notch:

"He saved my soul... He saved my soul... He saved my soul, He's so good... to... me..."

But it still wasn't enough, and I knew it. God deserved my all, every bit, every bit of volume and every ounce of power from every fiber of my being.

So I let it rip.

"He's coming soon... He's coming soon... He's coming soon, He's so good…to...

I would have finished the verse, really I would have, but apparently my God had heard all He needed to hear! For Paul and Silas He sent an earthquake. For me it was something just about as dramatic. When that cannonball landed just outside that shack, it absolutely wrecked it. Walls went flying, the roof went flying, supplies went flying...and I stood in the middle of it all, still, safe...and stunned. I heard myself saying over and over again, "He did it! God did it! He really did it!" And I probably would have kept on standing there and kept on saying it if two blurred figure had not raced past me, grabbed me by the hands, and dragged me with them.

"Yeah, Bro, He did it. Now could you please shut your yap and run faster? PLEASE?"

It was Carrie and Aly.

Chapter Thirteen

We raced through the forest woods of Chickamauga at break neck speed, and it was only the hand of God that kept us safe. Bullets and cannonballs were whizzing and wooshing, soldiers were charging and falling back, there was no human way possible that we could have survived being in the middle of it all.

Yet we did.

It must have been half an hour later that we finally stopped and collapsed, utterly exhausted. We found the dead fall of a massive old oak. The roots were sticking up in the air at least ten feet high, and the vines of the woods had started to form a virtual tent over the gap between the roots, the trunk, and the ground. We crawled underneath that

Heaven-sent shelter, laid on our backs, gasped for air, and said nothing for a good long while.

Finally, I found the breath to speak. My wonder at being delivered had faded and was slowly being replaced by a feeling of failure. What good was it to escape alive when we were still no closer to saving the Cape boys?

"I'm sorry, guys, this has not worked out very well so far."

That brought a rather strange reaction from Carrie and Aly. And by strange I mean that they looked at each other, grinned, then both looked at me and laughed!

"You don't know, do you?

"Don't know what, Carrie? Could you possibly put an object with that verb?"

She just grinned even bigger. "Bro, your off-key singing saved Patrick's life, at least for now, not to mention ours."

Now that got my attention!

"What are you talking about?"

"While you were in your own personal prison in that shack, we were at the cook wagon about fifty yards away. Two soldiers came by us, messengers from your buddy General Longstreet."

That made me growl, but she ignored me and kept going.

"They were talking about us, and wondering why the General was sending for Patrick Cape, and what he could want with him. Apparently, he wanted to find out why you were asking for him. A few minutes later they came back with him. Right about the time they came back by us, someone shouted for everyone to take up arms, and that there was a cannon being lit. Bro, I looked across the way, and I could see the flame of the fuse. I kid you not, it was aiming right at all of us that were around the cook wagon, including Patrick, me, and Aly. But at the last minute it swung to the right, and took dead aim at the prison shack! I just knew you were a goner. That ball hit not 30 feet from you! God is good, Bro. Any closer and you would have been gone along with that shack."

"Pretty amazing, I think," Aly said with a grin. "I knew your singing was bad, but now you hold the world record. I am pretty sure no one has ever sung bad enough to have someone shoot a cannon at them! And just think! From now on, every time you read about the Battle of Chickamauga, you'll know what the rest of the world never will: you started it!"

"Oh, your reeeeeal funny, Squirt," I said with a grin. But inwardly I was doing more than grinning. Inwardly I was smiling ear to ear. I wasn't at all sure that Carrie and Aly knew what they were talking about, I figured it was just a coincidence that the cannon man had changed direction like that. But however or even why it happened, at least now I knew that Patrick had survived the initial stages of the battle.

"We better get to sleep," I said, "and catch our ride home. Assuming that Patrick and George survived the rest of the battle, we'll still have to be ready to keep both of them from killing each other again tomorrow. After that, we should be good. The Battle of Chickamauga only lasted for two days, so if we succeed tomorrow, we shouldn't even have to come back on our day five."

With that, we nestled back up under the canopy of vines and drifted off to sleep.

Chapter Fourteen

Once again we woke up to very modern sounds. My eyes were still closed, but my ears were hearing the traffic on the road out in front of the hotel, the slamming of car doors in the parking lot, the humming of the hot water heater, and the muffled sound of a television from some room near to us.

I blinked a few times, rubbed my eyes, and realized that the lights were already on in the room. I could hear the shower now, and realized that someone, probably one of the girls, was in there getting ready for the day.

It didn't take long for all of us to be up, washed, dressed, and down in the lobby for breakfast. Then it was into the Yukon once more for the quick trip to Bible Baptist.

There was certainly no let down in the services. The Bible Baptist youth choir sang, and it felt like we were going to go to Heaven right there on the spot! Then there were some special numbers, and then Brother Alan Kirk preached. That is a big man with a big heart for God, and it always comes through clear in his messages. Then we heard from Stinnet Ballew again, then an awesome message from Dean McNeese, who is from right nearby in Ringgold.

That brought us up to lunch time. No disappointment there! The fellowship hall was jam slam packed, and the food was out of this world. We got to sit with a gentleman named Lance Carpenter. He is a singer, a really good one, and as we sat with him and listened to him talk to folks, one thing became very clear: he really loves the Lord a whole bunch!

Once we finished up lunch, it was back into the auditorium for more. We heard messages from James Jones, Mark Stroud, and Bobby Barnes.

We had a couple of hours to kill after that, so we all went back to the hotel to rest up for a bit. Then it was right back to church for supper and right back into the auditorium for more singing and preaching. The Daugherty Family sang; they are from Pascagoula, Mississippi. When the pastor told us that, I couldn't help but giggle a little. I didn't mean to, since it is really impolite to be giggling in church, but as soon as he said "Pascagoula," I could hear Ray Stevens voice in my head going "The day the squirrel went berserk, in the First Self Righteous Church, in that sleepy little town of Pascagoula..."

If you have never heard that song, you REALLY need to get it and listen to it. Absolutely hilarious!

Anyway, where was I? Oh yeah, I remember now. After the singing, dad preached a message on Simon of Cyrene called "The Man at the Other End of the Cross." It is really amazing to think of that man unexpectedly being called upon to carry the back end of the cross of Jesus.

When he was done, Tony Hutson preached. His messages are hard to outline, but they are also hard to forget!

After service we hung around and fellowshipped for a while, then we went out to a local restaurant with some of the other preachers and their families. We had already eaten supper earlier, but this gave us time to have some appetizers and dessert and just enjoy some sweet fellowship. Dad spent a lot of time talking to a great preacher by the last name of Bailey. It was either Chad or Brad, I'm not sure which since they are twins, and both pastors! I'm sure dad knew, but I didn't.

Finally it was back to the hotel for the night. Tooth-brushing, pajama-dressing, hugging, praying, lights out.

And right back on.

Chapter Fifteen

Light, lots of light. The sun was up and bright over the gunpowder haze of Chickamauga. It was sort of eerie, really. There was little noise to be heard and even less movement to be seen.

I knew that was not going to last.

The second day of the Battle of Chickamauga was supposed to start dark and early. Not bright and early, mind, you, dark and early. I knew from our research that General Bragg gave orders for the battle to start around 5:30 in the morning. But a series of miscommunications would end up delaying the start of the battle by about four hours. That delay was going to prove costly for them, but it may just be solid gold for us.

I sat up in the back of the wagon, and the Conductor just smiled and nodded.

"So what's the plan, Big Bro?" Aly asked with her standard mischievous grin.

I had been thinking of that, and I knew what we needed to do. I knew, but even I shook my head as I prepared to say it. We needed to keep at least one brother out of the way until today's battle was over. By then, everything would be safe, and it would be mission accomplished for us. I knew that the Confederates were going to win today, and win big. But our purpose was to save one or two specific lives, not to have anything to do with the battle. But how to do that? I knew, at least in general, and it was time to let the girls in on my plan. With something this crazy, I figured I better not sugar coat it, the blunt approach would be best.

"We are going to kidnap Patrick Cape."

That brought a moment of stunned silence from the girls. Finally, it was Carrie that broke the silence.

"Uh, Kyle, no offense, but are you COMPLETELY OUT OF YOUR MIND?"

I shushed her, motioning my hands downward to get her to be quiet and settle down. I didn't want to draw any undo attention, especially since we had very little time to work with.

"No, Sis, I don't think I am. In fact, I think this plan makes perfect sense. This is the last day of the battle. If we can just keep him out of it, everything should be fine. By late tonight the battle will be over, and the Federals will be on the run. They will head for Chattanooga, where the war will soon turn again in their favor. But for now, one day of success for us will mean life for George and Patrick."

"Yeah, yeah, yeah, I get that part," Carrie said dismissively, "it's that part about kidnaping a soldier in the middle of a war zone that strikes me as insane. Exactly how do you plan on doing that without getting us all killed, or getting yourself thrown in jail again?"

"How do you catch any big fish?" I answered with what I was pretty sure was a sly smile. Then I answered my own question, "the same way you catch a small fish. With bait."

"Bait. Riiiiiight."

That was Aly. She did not seem to be at all convinced.

"Yes, bait," I said. "Now, how about giving me a piece of paper and a pencil?"

Ever since our very first mission, West Virginia, we knew to carry things with us as we went to bed each night. Whatever we had in bed with us in our time somehow came with us back into the past. Aly reached into her knapsack that she had slept with and pulled out a piece of paper and a pencil. I got Carrie to turn away from me, and then I used her back as a desk to write my bait letter. A couple of minutes later I was done.

"There," I said, "that should do the job."

Carrie straightened up and said, "Well, what does it say?"

"Here, read it for yourself."

She reached out and took it, scanned over it, and said, "Well, maybe. It just might work, maybe."

"What? What does it say?" Aly said with a huff. She never liked to be left out of anything. Carrie handed it to her, and Aly read it aloud:

" 'Patrick, please come at once. It is in regards to your mother. The conversation that you and George had three days ago in the house with her has caused an unexpected and dramatic turn of events. If you do not come at once, all will be lost.' Yeah, that should work," she said, "and it is all true, even though we could never explain it to him. The unexpected and dramatic turn of events is us out here on the battlefield, no doubt, and it is certainly true that all will be lost unless we get him out of harm's way. And his mom certainly does need him to come home! Nice job."

"Thank you very much. Now we just have one other thing to deal with, and that is how to get the message to him!"

"Uh, yeah," Carrie said slowly, "there is that. But there is also the question of the kidnaping part. If we get him the letter and he runs home, then finds out his mom didn't send the letter, he'll just run right back to the battle. How do you intend to get the letter to him, and how do you intend to keep him at home?"

"As to the first part, I am not going to get the letter to him, you are."

"Whoa, whoa, whoa!" Carrie shouted. "Why me?"

"Because," I grinned, "me batting my eyelashes won't have near the same effect as you batting yours."

"And what is that supposed to mean? Have you forgotten that I am twelve?"

"No, Sis, but have you forgotten that it is 1863? You look fifteen or sixteen, and in this time period, you are practically an old maid at that age. Now pucker up, Buttercup, you have a letter to take to your beau."

Oh man, the glare that one earned me! I am pretty sure she would have slugged me if this weren't so important.

We knew pretty well by now where Patrick and his regiment would be. History is nice like that. We knew we could get to within a half mile or so without being noticed, so we told the Conductor where we needed to go, and we were off.

Half an hour later the wagon faded away from us into the trees once again. We knelt to pray, and then it was back up and on to the business at hand. Aly and I were going to wait just inside the tree line. Carrie would make the delivery. We knew that once she handed him the note, if he took the bait, he would first have to let his division commander know that he needed to be gone for "a few minutes." We would have a head start to his house, and when he got there, we intended on turning a few minutes into the entire day.

"I cannot believe I am doing this," Carrie said as she shook her head. "Boys are...so...boys!"

"Ouch, Sis," I said as I feigned an offended look. "That hurts!"

"I'm going to make sure it hurts a lot worse somewhere down the line. You will pay for this, I promise."

Then she turned from us, and walked out into the open toward men and boys lining up for war.

Chapter Sixteen

This is Carrie, and I'll take it from here. I really disliked my brother at that moment, but I knew he was probably right, this was about our only chance. But how in the world was I supposed to do this? I knew absolutely nothing about being "alluring." I am twelve, for goodness sake, the thought of boys was the farthest thing from my mind! Dad says that he intends for it to be that way for both Aly and I until we are a more reasonable age, say, 50ish. I am pretty sure he is kidding, at least a little bit.

Anyway, as I walked, I kept trying to think of how to act, but for the life of me I just couldn't come up with anything.

And then it hit me. Mom!

My mom has this way about her, especially with Dad. I often wonder if he realizes how much of a lump of putty he is in her pretty hands! She can look at him, smile a really amazing kind of a smile, tilt her head just so, laugh a low kind of laugh, and suddenly Mr. Macho is melting like a snow cone on a summer sidewalk! If I could just mimic her, maybe this would work!

As I approached where I knew the Confederate line in this area was, a harsh voice shouted out, "Halt! Who goes there?"

Really? Halt, who goes there? Who actually talks like that?

Anyway, I figured I better answer, and I figured it better sound good.

"Carrie Warner," I said in my best North Carolina lilt. "I need to see Patrick Cape, at once."

A moment of silence ensued, and then I saw two young men get up from behind the wood and earthworks barricade and approach me. They both had rifles. Both of them were pointing them at me. Rude!

I held my hands up in what I hoped was a non-threatening way and held very still till they reached me.

"Come with us," the taller one said brusquely.

Since they had guns, and since I wanted to go that way anyway, I did. If I hadn't wanted to go, I wouldn't have. I don't like being ordered around. My dad or my pastor or anyone else in a position of legitimate authority I will obey in a split second. But bully boys just make me mad. When I get married it will be to someone tough but tender like my dad, not to some ogre who thinks he is tough just because he is male.

In just a couple of minutes I was in the center of the camp. Everything was as tense as a fiddle string. I figure there was maybe another hour or so till the battle would start, I just hoped we could get everything done by then.

A few minutes later, I saw him. It was definitely Patrick. One of the bully boys was bringing him my way, and I could read his lips as he said, "You're sweetheart is here for you!"

If I couldn't keep from throwing up, I hoped that I could at least do so down that guy's boot leg.

But I knew I had to think more like mom and less like me right now. I put on my best "mom for dad" kind of smile, cocked my head just so and batted my eyes a couple of times right as they got to me.

"Miss, are you well? I don't know you, but you seem to have something wrong with your face."

Oh thanks, Patrick, I thought to myself, now my confidence is really soaring...

I handed him the letter, and lost the goofy look on my face.

"Patrick, you must come at once. This letter will explain everything."

Then I turned and left, at a very quick walk. I didn't want to be detained.

"Sir, she's leaving, shall I stop her?"

I recognized that voice as bully boy number two. It was Patrick who answered, "No, she's just a girl; what harm can she do?"

Ouch! Now I could feel my face getting red and my ears getting hot! So help me, if I got out of this alive, I would make Kyle pay for this!

Once I got past the line and out of sight, I ran like a rabbit. A couple of minutes later I slid back into the woods where Kyle and Aly were waiting. Kyle jumped out with wide eyes and said, "Well? Did it work? Did he take the bait?"

I don't recommend physical violence on most occasions. But I could not help but grab my rotten brother by the collar and yank him nose to nose with me as I said, very threateningly, "If you ever put me in a situation like that again, I will show Helen Douglas the baby pictures of you in the tub with your shiny hiney up in the air. Are we clear on that?"

He turned really white, shook his head up and down very slowly, and said, "Crystal clear." Knowing your brother's curly headed blonde crush has its advantages.

Then we ran.

As we bolted down trails, around dead falls, and over hills, Kyle explained his idea for part two of today's plan. I could see Aly shaking her head and grinning. She thought it was great, which meant that it was probably going to end up getting us into a ton of trouble.

Chapter Seventeen

This is Kyle, I'll pick it back up from here.

As we approached the house, we slid to a stop, hit the ground, and looked for any signs of movement. Then we backed up into the trees just a bit and got set up.

There was a path, very well worn, and we knew it was the one always traveled to and from the house. When Patrick came, he would be in a huge hurry if he reacted to the letter like we figure he would. He would not likely be looking down at his feet as he ran, and therefore he would not see the wire.

I had carried some thin, high tensile wire with me to bed last night, borrowed from my dad's tool kit in the back of the Yukon. There are four things you can always count on my dad having handy: Duct Tape, WD40, electrical tape, and wire. He says, "If you need to make it be still, use Duct Tape. If you need to make it move, use WD40. If you need to make it stop bleeding, use electrical tape. If you need to hang it up, use wire."

I took a piece about 15 feet long, picked out two sturdy looking trees on either side of the path, and set to work. I strung the wire incredibly tight between them, and about six inches off of the ground. I handed Aly a toboggan, which for those who do not know is a hat kind of thing that you can pull all the way down onto your head, or even over a face if need be. I gave Carrie a bandanna and some short lengths of rope.

We took up positions behind trees just a few feet ahead of the trip wire. That's the great thing about old growth forests, the trees are big enough to hide behind without being seen!

Sooner than we expected, we heard footsteps running down the path, coming our way in a big hurry. Patrick was clearly taking this very seriously. That would help, it would keep him from paying close attention. I figured the trip wire was bound to work on him.

Boy, did it ever! He had to be going top speed when his foot hit it, and he went sprawling like a maniac, face first onto the ground!

We didn't hesitate. We were on our third mission now, and we were confident enough just to do what needed to be done. When he hit the ground, I was instantly out from behind the tree and onto his back. Ordinarily, he probably would have been very hard to handle. But when he hit the ground we could hear him go, "Ooooof!" as all the wind got knocked out of him. He was pretty much helpless. I grabbed his arms and pulled them up behind his back. Carrie tied his hands very tightly together, and at the very same time Aly twisted up the bandanna, put it in his mouth, and tied it behind his head to keep him quite.

Quick as a flash Carrie was down onto his legs, and tied his feet together. At the exact same time Aly had pulled the toboggan down over his head and face, where he could not see. Then we all sat on his back for just a moment and tried to catch our own breath! The whole capture had taken less than 60 seconds, and we were really huffing.

Finally I said, "Ok, it's time to move him. If we stay here, we are likely to be found by some troops from one side or the other. That wouldn't be good. Let's get him into the barn. I guarantee that his mom will be on her knees in prayer this entire day, pouring out her heart to God. We should be able to carry him into the barn without her ever noticing. Then we sit and wait out the day, and we have accomplished our mission."

We got Patrick up onto his feet, and tied up as he was and still half out of breath, he didn't have any struggle in him yet. That was good, I needed him to be still while I hoisted him up.

Every boy ought to be more concerned with his back and biceps more than with his thumbs. Most kids play games all day, but a better use of time is things like chopping wood and hauling brush. Dad made sure I worked and played hard enough to be as strong as most men already. I was really glad of that as I bent Patrick over and hoisted him up over my shoulders in the fireman's carry. He was heavy. Not for my dad, maybe, but definitely for me.

We made our way through the woods, out behind the barn, said a quick and silent prayer, then bolted for the barn through the back entrance.

We made it safely in.

Aly found a stool in a stall, and she set it up in a corner. I put Patrick down onto it, and by now he was starting to squirm and struggle some. We tied his legs and hands to the stool itself, and once we were confident that he could not get loose, we took off the toboggan. I wouldn't have liked being blindfolded all day; I figured he wouldn't either. Besides, by this point it wouldn't matter if he saw us. All we had to do was keep him here till nightfall and we would have accomplished our mission!

Patrick just glared at us, a really angry kind of look.

"Bro," Carrie said, "It wouldn't hurt for us to talk to him, you know, and remind him about what is important. What could it hurt? We can be careful in what we say."

I thought about that for a minute, and finally came to the conclusion that she was right.

"Patrick," I said, "you don't know us, and really, it doesn't matter who we are. All you need to know is that we are friends, to you, to your brother George, and to your mom. Think about it. If we were enemies, we could have killed you already, right?"

He looked at me, hard, and then his face softened just a touch. I could tell he was thinking about it.

"It doesn't matter *how* I know, but this is *what* I know. I know that both you and your brother have been called to preach. I know that there is no greater or higher calling in the world than that. You have gotten all distracted by the need to defend your home. Your brother has gotten all distracted by the need to stop slavery. As good as those two things are, they don't hold a candle to the need to preach the gospel. Jesus said, 'Go ye into all the world, and preach the gospel to every creature.'

"That calling is the most important thing for you and for your brother, you have both just forgotten that. I believe that if you go back out into that battle, you or your brother or both will end up dead. The result of that will be who knows how many thousands of people dying without having received Jesus Christ as their Savior. Is that what you want?"

The look on his face was indescribable. A tear trickled down his cheek, and he hung his head. My heart broke for him. I went over to him, and put my hands on his slumping shoulders.

And then I felt myself having the breath knocked out of me! He headed butted me in the stomach and drove himself into me with his legs! He had played me, bad, with that tear on the cheek routine.

Carrie and Aly were there in an instant, rolling him off of me, with him trying to kick and squirm his way out of his restraints.

He wouldn't have any luck there, we knew how to tie knots.

We got him set back up in place, and then we tied the stool itself to a post behind it so he couldn't try that one again. I caught my breath, brushed myself off, and said, "Hoss, that's the last time I'll fall for that. It is real clear that you don't want to listen, so you can just sit and chill out instead. We have all day."

"Bro," Aly said with one cocked eyebrow, "I don't think he knows what it means to 'chill out.' "

"Ahh, you're probably right. Let's try this then," I said as I looked over at him firmly, "we're here to babysit, so sit, baby."

And sit we did, all of us, until sundown. We sat through a day of the nearby thunderings of cannons and muskets. Then we loosened the knots on his arms enough for him to eventually wiggle his way out, slipped out of the barn, into the forest, and bedded down for our nightly ride home.

Chapter Eighteen

When we woke up back in our time and in our hotel, I was really pleased. "Four days," I mumbled to myself. "We did it in only four day. We're getting pretty good at this."

"We sure did," Carrie mumbled back as she rolled over and looked down at the floor to face me. "But let's not get too cocky. In fact, let's not get cocky period. Remember, James 4:6 says 'God resisteth the proud, but giveth grace unto the humble.' Yeah, we got done in four days, but without God's help and strength, we would have surely failed."

"Agreed, Sis, agreed."

With the mission over, we settled in to enjoying ourselves on the last full day there in Rossville. We had breakfast, went back to Bible Baptist, and had ourselves a time. We got to hear Chris Hewitt sing again, then Chris Simpson preached. After him we got to hear Sammy Allen one more time. I know he is getting old, but I really hope he lives another fifty years. Joe Arthur preached, then we had lunch.

Once we finished lunch, we kicked around Rossville for a couple more hours, shopped a bit at some local thrift stores, then headed back to church. Pastor Barry Philbeck preached again, and then my dad preached one last time. Several more people got saved, and there was hardly a dry eye in the house.

After church we went out for some ice cream, fellowshipped with some of the preachers and their families, and talked till well into the night. Then it was back to the hotel. We got as much stuff packed as we could, and then settled in for the night. It would be nice to have an actual, real night's sleep. I took my Bible out, and read it by flash light for a good while, just because I love it and my Jesus who wrote it. And somewhere in the midst of reading and loving, I fell asleep.

Chapter Nineteen

Voices. Urgent voices. The smell of smoke. Shaking. Someone was shaking me. I could feel my Bible still in my right hand, right where it was when I fell asleep. Maybe the hotel was on fire. Wake up; I need to wake up!

Do you know that heart-racing feeling you get when something suddenly wakes you up out of a sound sleep? My heart was racing like that. Something was wrong, very badly wrong.

I jerked straight up in bed. But I was not in bed, and it was not dark. And it was not the twenty-first century either. It did not take a rocket scientist to figure this out. The back of the wagon, the Conductor sitting up front and looking back at me with a worried look on his face, the haze of gunpowder. The mission that was over? It wasn't over.

"It is urgent that you wipe the sleep out of your eyes and shake the cobwebs out of your head," the Conductor said as seriously as a graveyard. "As you and your sisters and I myself have obviously learned, the mission is not over, and the Cape brothers are still at risk. The Battle of Chickamauga is over, but it seems that one or the other of the Cape brothers is still intent on killing the other, otherwise you three would not still be here."

"Where? Where are they? Where do we look?"

"I do not know," he said. "That is your decision. But whatever you do, you must do quickly."

"The house," Aly shouted. "Take us to the house. The boys have just come through a battle and seen many of their friends blown to bits. They will want to go somewhere familiar to them, somewhere they have known since they were little. It is what I would do. If anyone will know that place, their mom will."

Without a second of hesitation the Conductor slapped the reins and the donkey started running. The Conductor drove like a man possessed, and the donkey pulled like a race horse. We went sliding around curves, whipping through low hanging branches, and suddenly burst out into the open right by the farm house.   The Conductor yanked the wagon to a stop, and all three of us Night Heroes piled out at once. We went running to the door and banged on it with no hint of subtlety. Lives were at stake; we had no time to be subtle.

Very quickly the door opened, and we were face to face again with Mama Cape. Before she could speak, I did.

"Ma'am, I hate to be so abrupt, but your boy's lives are at risk, and we are here to save them. You have been praying, we are the answer. But we need your help. I am asking you to trust us, though you do not really know us. We need to come in, and we need to come in right now, this instant."

Mrs. Cape was stunned, but amazing woman that she was, she threw the door open wide and said, "Come right in and tell me what you need."

We quickly sat down around the table, and I tried to very quickly explain without giving away any forbidden details.

"Ma'am, for your sons, the battle is not yet over. Their anger is eating them alive, and we are certain that one of them is going to try to hunt down and kill the other this very day. We need to know what special place they both know, a place they would have been familiar with since they were very young."

She was horrified, and her face went ashen white. But she kept her composure and within a split second had the answer we needed.

"There is a valley about two miles west of here, with a high rocky bluff overlooking it. There is a grove of four or five very old oak trees in the center of that valley. The boys played there almost every day while they were growing up. If either of them is troubled in mind, that is where he will go."

Without a further word, we immediately jumped up and ran for the door, but she stopped us in our tracks, just for a second, with one last word. "Please, whoever you are, save my boys."

"We will, ma'am, we will, or we will die trying."

Then we bolted out the door.

Chapter Twenty

We ran, oh boy, did we run. We had to find that valley and bluff, and we had to find it immediately. How could we have missed this? How could we not have known that one of them would not care that the battle was over? How could we not have known that the devil would still be at work?

It took us about twenty minutes to get to the edge of the forest overlooking the valley. We slid to a stop, looked down into the center, and saw the trees Mrs. Cape had told us about. There, sitting down in front of one, was Patrick Cape. He looked like he was reading a book, maybe something to try and clear his head.

We looked off to the side and saw a high rocky bluff. It had to be the one Mrs. Cape told us about.

"Aly, stay here and keep an eye on Patrick. If he moves, stop him; I don't care how you do it."

She grinned, and I knew she could and would do it. I hoped she didn't have to.

"Carrie, you head carefully up that bluff from this side. But give me ten minutes before you start up. I am going to loop around and come up from the other side, and it will take me at least that long to get there."

"What are we going to do when we get up there?"

"I don't know yet, we'll have to figure that out once we're there; there really isn't any time for planning."

And with that I took off on a run. My heart was racing a million miles an hour. We could not let this happen! No way were we going to fail when both lives and souls were at stake; no way were we going to let the devil have this kind of a victory.

Chapter Twenty-One

This is Carrie, I'll pick the story up from here. Once Kyle took off running, I carefully watched my watch. At exactly ten minutes I started up my side of the bluff. It was a bit rough, but I am not your average girl. Mom says I am pretty, dad says I am tough. Right now, I was going with dad.

I scrambled over rock and root, and within a few minutes was at the top. There was a decent sized plateau, and I could not help but gasp as I saw what I saw. There, right at the edge of the bluff, was George Cape. He was very calmly and carefully loading his rifle. He was big and had a determined look on his face. I could not handle him. Even Kyle would have a rough go of it.

He finished preparing his rifle, and I could not help but gasp under my breath as I saw him carefully lay it across a low hanging tree branch for support and aim it down into the valley. He was going to shoot his own brother!

I was paralyzed, not knowing what I could or should do.

George breathed in and out slowly, calming himself so as to make his shot perfect. Two or three more seconds and he would pull the trigger and end his brother's life. Suddenly there was a flash of movement from off to the right. It was Kyle!

Kyle came diving in at full speed, smashing right into his side. The gun went off, and both Kyle and he went tumbling over the edge of the hill—a fighting, grasping, undistinguishable mass of fists and feet...

I piled over the hill after them. Kyle may not be able to handle this guy, and I would fight him myself rather than let my brother get hurt. I slid down to the bottom, and all the way down I could hear Aly screaming something. I looked up, and she was kneeling over Patrick. Oh no, no, no, no!

At the bottom of the hill, I saw Kyle land on top of George and immediately rare back that big right arm of his. With a thundering crash, he brought it down onto George's jaw as he screamed one word at the top of his lungs:

"ENOUGH!"

And it was.   The valley fell silent, except for Aly.   She was sobbing, and that could not be good at all.

Chapter Twenty-Two

I rushed over to her and found that Kyle was right on my heels. Patrick was laying on his back, writhing, gasping. Aly was holding his arm and shoulder and saying over and over again, "Please be ok, please be ok, please be ok!"

And then came the biggest surprise of all. Right behind Kyle was George. He slid to a stop right beside Kyle, right over his brother. Kyle jumped up to fight him but quickly saw that it was not necessary.

"Patrick, brother, forgive me; I am so sorry! Oh, dear God of Heaven, what have I done! Forgive me, Father, forgive my blindness and hatred. Oh, dear God, please spare the life of my brother and take my foolish life instead!"

With that, he grabbed his brother by the coat and buried his head in his bosom, weeping like a baby.

I think we all heard the whisper at the same time. "Every word of God is pure: he is a shield unto them that put their trust in him, Proverbs 30:15. The Word of God has been my shield, George. If not, I would be dead, for your shot was very true, as it has always been."

We all stopped everything we were doing, whether it was crying or praying or pleading. "Patrick! Do you yet live? My shot was aimed for your head, this young man slamming into me altered the shot, yet it still pierced your chest. How are you still alive?"

There was utter silence, as we all looked down at Patrick, who was obviously alive. We gasped as he reached into his coat, and pulled out a Bible.

"I had just finished reading and put it back in my coat to go home. I needed some peace; I needed some answers. I did not know that this book would save my life today as it saved my soul years ago."

We looked at the cover, and right through the B of the word Bible, there was a bullet hole. Patrick shook his head, and opened that old Bible, a beautiful, worn, tattered old thing, and let it fall open to the page where the bullet had stopped.

I guess God really is perfect in all that He does. The bullet stopped right on Matthew 5:24. All of us smiled and shook our heads, and it was George who read it aloud:

"Be reconciled to thy brother."

He looked at Patrick, and we Night Heroes all looked at each other. Last night we thought it, but now we knew it.

Mission accomplished.

Coming Soon

The Night Heroes Book Four

The Blade of Black Crow

Tears of fear were streaming down Aly's face. Mine too. Kyle and Black Crow circled each other warily. I knew my brother was strong, really strong, but that knife in Black Crow's hand was gleaming and razor sharp. Everything was at stake for Black Crow; if Kyle won, he would never be chief. That being the case, Black Crow would not hesitate to kill...

Meet the Author

Dr. Wagner is the founder and pastor of Cornerstone Baptist Church of Mooresboro, North Carolina. He was saved in 1979 and began preaching regularly as a twelve-year-old boy in 1982.

He earned an Associate's Degree in Communications Technology from Cleveland Community College in 1989. He earned his Bachelor's Degree in Pastoral Studies with highest honors in 1997 and then his Master's and Doctorate with highest honors from Carolina Bible College in 2001 and 2003. He founded Cornerstone Baptist Church in 1997. He has been teaching at the Carolina Bible College since 2000 and has been a professor since 2003.

He has been writing books since 2009, with Cry from the Coal Mine being his first fiction book.

Along with pastoring, Dr. Wagner preaches in many revivals, camp meetings, and family conferences each year.

He married Dana in 1994. They have three children: Caleb, Karis, and Aléthia.

Other Books in the Night Heroes Series

Cry From the Coal Mine

Free Fall

The Blade of Black Crow
(Coming soon)

9 781941 039991